For

Girlfriends

Written and Illustrated
by
Synthia Saint James

PETER PAUPER PRESS, INC.
WHITE PLAINS, NEW YORK

For my best girlfriend

Text copyright © 1997
Peter Pauper Press, Inc.
202 Mamaroneck Avenue
White Plains, NY 10601
Illustrations copyright © 1997
Synthia Saint James
All rights reserved
ISBN 0-88088-229-8
Printed in Singapore
7 6 5 4 3 2 1

Girlfriends

Contents

Introduction

A true girlfriend is a sister girl
That's got your back
Is in your corner
And by your side
Whenever you need her.

What a special gift! Backing each
other, talking, confiding . . . sharing our
private thoughts and to-be-realized
dreams . . .

A true girlfriend is a sister girl
That's me
And that's you!

S. S. J.

Sister Girl
to
Sister Girl

On the day of your birth the sun must have shined brighter as it smiled upon us all. And the air was probably filled with the aroma of fresh spices. You are sun-shine's child then and now filled with the delight you share with us all.

You came into this life with a rainbow array of ideas, creativity and strong convictions. And I feel blessed knowing that I call you girlfriend.

Together we've shared all kinds of times
From laughing to crying and all those in-between times
Sometimes the laughter came right after crying
Or we laughed so hard that we ended up crying.

When I first saw you, way back in those early days, I knew then that you would become my best girlfriend.

Our first high school dance
Our knobby knees knocking against
the other
Wearing our first high heel pumps of
patent leather
Complete with our new dressy dresses
Standing there wondering,
Would one of us be asked to dance.

Our first major crush
He seemed so very tall then
But we know now that he never would
reach
A man's average height
But he was definitely dark and lovely
We took turns calling him by phone

But neither of us could muster even
a hello
So he never heard anything except a
dial tone
Or maybe the sound of two very silly
girls giggling.

Today, just another day, girlfriend you
never know what exactly is in store. You
go through another day filled with hopes,
maybe even promises. But living tomorrow
can't be promised, live for today.

I'd hate it if we were too much alike.
For then, what could we give each other?

I cry, you cry. It's a release, that's all, a
release.

Learning to scream, something we all need to know how to do. If we hold all that screaming energy inside, it will ruin our insides. We need our insides!

You've got it going on! Sure you do! Sure you do! Good black don't crack. But "Good Black" comes in many shades, from savory tan to deep dark chocolate. All you need is some African descent.

My biggest hope and desire is just for you to know that I'm behind you. Even if it's up a lifetime creek.

Girl, you know, when times were hard you were always there spending time helping me. It didn't matter if it was day or night or even if I got you up out of your bed, you always came running.

A girlfriend, sister girl, is a person that you may hate to awaken at any given hour, night or day. But your friendship is so deep that she'd be mad if you didn't.

Weren't you cute . . . all dressed up in your running suit. Ready and willing to run our on-going, relentless battle of good times, good food, love and excitement and always thinking we need to lose weight. When did we forget that beauty comes in all sizes?

Time just seems to pass by so quickly. That old saying "I remember you when" comes to mind. How great it's been sharing adventures!

I am sending you all the fresh healing fruits for both body and soul, sprinkled with all the sweetness of our friendship.

Yeah girl, I know, it has been years. But I can see you now and for as long as I can remember, new hat, dress, shoes and a big wide smile, strutting to church Sunday mornings.

Girlfriend, thanks for being there
To always help heal all life's bruises.

Sister girl thank you for being part of my world.

The Beauty Shop

Now what about those special beauty shop magicians? Mine, her name is Alannah, and she Alannahsizes me. Never an important event, in or out of town that I don't see her first. Then refreshed and just feeling wondrous, there's nothing I can't feel good about after leaving her salon.

Sitting in the beauty shop watching all the girlfriends coming in. Some with scarves, others in hats or caps. Always leaving with their heads held high and with a definite lift to their posture.

So many different hairstyles, colors and tints. So many different shapes, sizes and ages. All very proud black sisters with so many places to go and always so very much to do.

The shop is the place to catch up on all things. What's going on? Where've you just been? Where are you going? Who's

with who? Oh please girl, excuse me.
You're telling me. I can't believe my ears.

So many magazines to browse through
catching up on the tee. Like *Ebony, Jet,
Black Elegance, Upscale, Black Hair* and
you know now there's plenty of stories
on us in *People*.

Then there's the radio playing our grooves,
old and new. And the smells of all the
shampoos, conditioners, the hot comb, all
sorts of perfumes and colognes mixed with
the many scents of my sisters.

No matter where the sister lives, she
comes to the 'hood when the time comes
to get her hair done.

The beautician is a confidante, a
bartender of hair.

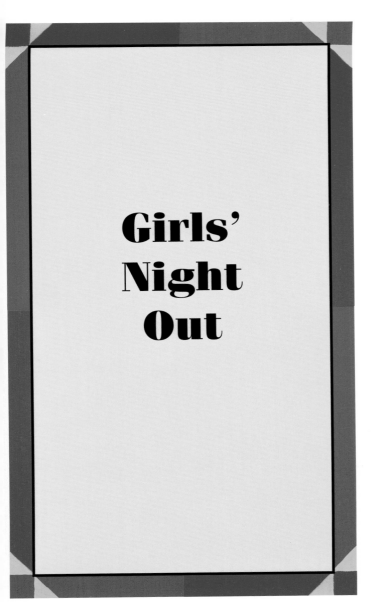

Girls' Night Out

As far as I'm concerned, every night is girls' night. That is especially, every night I decide to go out.

Now about dinner, it's my treat. Shall we do Italian, Chinese, French, or Japanese? Or better yet, how about that down home, downstairs, jazzy, basement place?

Isn't it nice to sit back and relax in a bar or restaurant? Laugh and talk, kick your heels up or kick them off. Catch up on small or even deep talk?

Red. Now that's a color I only wear when I feel like strutting my stuff. Heh sister girl, are you up to something?

Girl, don't even look up. Don't even try to
guess just who's at the door. Right now
I'm trying very hard to make magic, like in
just disappear.

A person, he or she, nothing but a piece of
clay with a microphone. When you find
that they do you more harm than good,
just cut off the speaker.

Heh, don't you dare go there
You've got too much to offer
To waste time dwelling on any fool.

Yeah, love is out there. It's that matter of
time we go through to find it. "It" as in the
everlasting kind.

Just
Being
Girlfriends

Girlfriend, girlfriend, come on girl, pick
up the phone. You've got to be there.
Sister girl, I've got some juicy news
for you.

Excuse me, what did you just say? Try and
just say it to my face. You know gossip is
very very ugly! And you know, God don't
like ugly!

I heard they've got a major sale going on,
over at that new mall. Two for the price of
one on everything. Covering you from
head to toe. Let's go!

Check out our mirror images.
Decked out in new hats and new dresses.
Looking sharp with just a hint of sassy.
Girl, that color sure looks good on you!

You know, things are going really great!
Let's cook dinner tonight. You know like
our specialties. You cook your peas and
rice and I'll do my cod fish supreme. Heh,
I've got someone coming over I'm sure
you'll like.

Now I appreciate you girl, but why did you
have to go and do that. You know I hate
blind dates and you want me to cook too.
Oh, all right. I guess it couldn't hurt. I've
got nothing to do tonight. Do you still
have any cans of my coconut milk? Okay,
I'll stop and get some on the way. What
time did you say? Okay, okay, okay . . .

Let's have an old fashioned hen party, just
us girls. Let's fix a way down home meal.
Like collard greens, macaroni and cheese,
fried chicken wings with biscuits smoth-
ered in brown gravy. It will be a meal
straight from Grandma's kitchen but
topped with champagne. So what do
you say?

A Sister
and
Her Man

Yeah, I agree, he is cute
But what you see is not always
What you get.

Girlfriend, you have to just summon the
strength to be you. You'll be amazed,
proud and happy at what really just being
you will do.

Yeah, I've been through that, girl. How
easily said when that hurt has already
begun to subside. But how about when
that hurt has just begun? How do you
get through those days and especially
those nights?

I'm absorbing all that you're saying and doing. Although it may not be noticeable, I've been considering it all.

To enjoy someone truly, you cannot try and possess them. For that would smother out whatever existing flame they lighted your spark with.

I know that Cheshire cat grin of yours. And believe me I can see your blush. Now since when have you come into the office all hush hush?

A hair appointment? Now that's been twice in one week. Only last month it was once every other week. There's something you're not telling.

Used to be, I couldn't ever get you off the phone. But here lately I can't even reach you at home. What's up girlfriend, you've been avoiding this too long. Okay, but at lunchtime you better fess up.

Hummmmmmmmm! Sounds good to me. Now he does what for a living? How and where did you meet him? Where did you say he lives? You're going away for the weekend? Are you sure he's not married? Then why all the secrecy?

Yeah, he sounds like something pretty special. Now sister, please keep your eyes wide open. No, I'm not trying to put a damper on it. Of course I'm happy for you. Just remember I've only your best interest at heart.

You go girl, you sure better go!
I heard all about your good news.
You go girl, you sure better go!

Coupling

Coupling, our natural instinct. Other times a brought-on pain.

A love affair has many stages. The beginning bubbling scintillation, usually called infatuation. Few get past this initial situation. With time comes learning, possible deepening of affection. With time also, what was once had can so easily be lost. A fling some call it. It's healthy and well warranted. But time, as always, tells all.

Fighting is hard, giving is easy. But when you've been fighting for so long, it's harder to give. It may take a little more time, but I feel strongly, you'll be a giver again.

Distance sees what closeness can't.

I choose not to be confused
But to understand.

I now realize that love is not, and does
not require, masochism. For to love, you
must first love and continue to love
yourself, first.

If love were made totally to depend on the
love object, then what could possibly be
retained for one's own necessities?

We go through only what we put
ourselves through.

I find myself searching. For what I'm not
sure. A tremendous yearning, a need for
more. Something that for me must be
necessary. A need, but maybe even more.

I spoiled you, therefore I asked for what
I got.
Have you ever fixed your mouth to make
that statement?

Girl, let me tell you something
He was just what the doctor ordered
And just what the French chef prepared
Double Dutch chocolate and then some
So I ordered a second helping.

Girl, I said to him:
Just who do you think you are?
That you feel you can walk into my life
Out of nowhere, and control my destiny.

I'm the quickest fool when it comes to
making them superhuman, place them
on pedestals. And I'm the first to cry,
when they can't maintain that position.
A position they didn't even ask for.

Like a broken pitcher, I feel. At the end of
each relationship that I pour my entire
contents into. But always I have found that
my repair shop is within my own mind.
And there, and only there will I find peace.
When I put him far from my mind, I
decide I'm not his, I'm mine. I find myself
lightheaded, dancing. . . . Until that time
that I find him missing.

Just coming out of a daze.
I look around, realize where I am now.
Who's missing from this place.
Who's not sharing my every day with me.
I try to express my feelings on the space of
a written page.

He was so good to me. How could I help but love him. It seemed I should, only to find out that the feelings weren't the love I thought I had, no not at all. He was there when I was in need. He fulfilled my desires. Yes, that's what it was, desires. I needed to be loved, made to feel important, fussed over and truly cared for. I was new to myself, and he was there with so much guidance and his very special kindnesses. My true feelings, oh, how to put them in words. I never felt false.

Girlfriend, I have something to tell you. I'm sure you saw it coming, but now I can say it. Love is the most beautiful feeling anyone could ever experience! Yeah, I know you know that, just give me a minute, I feel poetic. I'm in love! It feels good to say it! I'm not only capable of love. I'm in love! There I said it again.

Today I feel love. I'm a surging sea, my ocean welled up inside of me. When my time comes I'll call my tide forth, my body then laid to rest on shore. When daybreak calls, my time to recede, back I'll call my waters, back inside of me. Here they'll await the time, when again I'll release this massive billow swelling within me. Today I feel loved, love returned, its energy creating intensity much like steam propelling a ship, vapor causing mobility. Today I feel love. Today I feel loved. Its power has overwhelmed me.

Achieving

Didn't you see all those beautiful black sisters, from many nations far and wide. Competing and winning gold, silver and bronze medals, or just included in a world-wide celebration of achievement for athletes. Inspiration to put our minds, bodies and souls into whatever our greater goals may be. Or do we need to rerun those tapes?

Now you can kick up your heels with joy. After so many years of dedicated hard work. You've earned a new rite of passage.

A Renaissance woman, a beacon, and a bright light, that's what you are.
Who will rise above and beyond most of life's challenges.
A Renaissance woman with so much to give and share.
With many friends who greatly care.

You've inherited a great mind, with the ability to learn, set goals and achieve, from the spirits of our African legacy.

Yes you can hold that chin up high. Smile so wide that you over-exercise those high cheek bones. Because you did it and all on your own.

There's a dim shining light,
Shining in my faint sight
That tells me I'm headed in the right direction.

Getting Ahead

Yeah girl, I decided to go back to school. Complete my college degree and then some, maybe even my Ph.D. There has always been more to life for me. Always more to accomplish and do . . . all the things I'm actually here for.

Opportunity, opportunity . . . a promise generally not kept, just something to lure you into a supposed higher job opportunity, opportunity, opportunity?

You know, girlfriend, we have to make our own opportunities based on our many different gifts. Take a few so-called risks, and go for it all, our own businesses.

Isn't it nice to wake up in the morning and know that you're in charge of your own destiny?

Of course sometimes and often we have to maintain a job or sometimes even more than one to get where we want to be, but as long as we have a place that we're going no matter how out of reach it may seem to be, we know we're going right there!

The Lowdown on Dough

Now girlfriend, let's just take a moment and discuss this phrase, "Money is the root of all evil." Now you know me and I know you, let's rephrase this together. "If you want to see an evil sister, just mess with her money."

This may be a community property state, but I didn't work hard, cook, clean and raise our kids to end up paying who, him, what, alimony . . .

What money means to me: freedom to be me.

Now we all know about stretching a dollar, but isn't it great when we can stretch it in our direction.

When I think of money, I think about our children and what we can give them that we probably didn't have, except by some possible miracle. My mission is to offer them greater knowledge and to develop their good sense.

She did *what* with her allowance? It must be time for her to start working for McDonald's or some other fast food chain.

Everything is due, as always. . . . We rob Peter to pay Paul, or Nordstrom instead of Macy's, that is if we're still single . . .

Money, money, money, you can't do with it and you can't do without it . . .

Family
Matters

Isn't it nice when things begin to seem to start working out on their own. Even though we know better. Yeah, we're back together. Sure you're right. You know you got it right. I know you've checked it out. Yeah, I've got my flow back but his is back too. And you know, our happiness is rubbing off on our children. Isn't that nice!

Do you know? Can you imagine? That man of mine, you know, my husband, cooked dinner for me tonight. The table was all candlelit and set with our best dishes. You know like in some kind of fancy restaurant. There wasn't even a special occasion that I knew of. Then he said the special occasion was our love.

So you heard I'm expecting a precious little miracle. Strapped to your back or on your lap, but always somewhere near. New sights, diapers and tiny clothing all about. New sounds, little cries, gurgles and laughs.

New smells, baby lotions, powders and creams. A new brown baby. A precious little miracle.

The kids are growing like weeds. Believe me I know. I find myself tilting my head back greatly just to say hello or sometimes having to raise myself up on tippy-toe.

Now look here, how many times do I have to tell you? I'm the only parent here. You are the child! I don't care what size shoes you wear. Once again, for your ears only, I'm the only parent here, you hear?

You know there was a time when a "good old fashioned beating" was the usual thing to keep children large and small in line? Now it's called abuse, please dial 911.

But know this clearly, I learned it when
I was very young, a punishment, like
depriving you of all your deemed normal
privileges, as in the use of the phone, etc.,
etc., or in younger days just going out to
play. What hurts more?

A surprise party? I can't believe it. Something given me by my family. I'm not sure
that I want to own up to my new special
age. Wasn't it nice that they didn't put it on
the cake. There'd be too many candles.

Yeah, we made it to the family reunion.
There was Mama Hattie, Cousin Rose,
Papa Joe, etc., etc. All together and
loving each other.

Isn't it nice when we put all past
grievances behind and enjoy just being
together, one big happy family.

Excuse me, now I know that Mr. Handsome is not about to lose his hair. Not Mr. Big Stuff. Well I'm sure that you'll somehow maintain your big head anyway. Teasing, I'll always love you, you'll always be my baby brother.

My mother's theme song for me and all of her children was to "keep on pushing," and I heeded those very special lyrics.

It's a proud thing when you walk down the street, or gather in a special place, just family, greeted as a unit. Oh, and isn't it great when people ask: "Is that your mother?" "I know he must be your father, must have spit you out."

But you know that family isn't always defined by bloodlines. It's about people you meet and the very special ancestors that help and allow you to be. Family by blood, family by support and friendship– I'm very lucky, girlfriend.

Reflections
on
Life

Yeah girl, I'm getting it all back together!

I saw myself from my outsides and there-fore began to understand my insides.

We all have to face the bad, then deal with it.

You know, sometimes we need to shed. At times it's hard. It actually hurts. But soon I'll be what's really me.

I need a quiet that is so loud, you can hear it shout.

Home is a place where relaxation should reign and peace of mind be obtained. Where patience can be defined as regroup-ing all the nerves we hold inside. But when this perfect space is impossible at times, isn't it great to have a friend to turn to?

Every day I learn more about myself. Exploring one's self is more important than finding something new around you. But then again, something new around you can help you find yourself too.

Life, full of second thoughts. Was there something I missed? Could there be something I'm missing? Did I make the right decision? Can I try it again?

I made my life easier, I stopped fighting me.

Adults, still children always testing how far they can go in many given situations . . .

The trick is not to place friends on pedestals. Not to try and classify what they will and will not do.

Since I started getting my outside exercise
clearing my head and letting out all that
stress, I began appreciating all the beauty
surrounding me.

To be with someone, man, woman or child,
makes you more aware of everything
around you.

When I decided not to run again, I left
myself wide open to whatever comes my
way and all the emotions, direct outcomes.
A big step, oh yes, could be scary I guess.
But it's a decision I've got to stick with.
I still feel attractive and desirable. I'm still
pursued. But one day I'll be old or, just sim-
ply put, older, for age is a true honor I hold
in the deepest reverence. It's eldership. But I
must continue to make my mark so something will be left. My sort of contribution to
our legacy. I never want for people to say,
what a beauty she used to be, what a
shame. But instead I'd love for them to look
at my work and say, she's beautiful!
Hopefully that will be my destiny.